presents . . .

Mark McGwire

MAC ATTACK!

by
Rob Rains

SPORTS PUBLISHING INC.
Champaign, IL 61820

Book design, editor: Susan M.
McKinney
Cover design: Julie L. Denzer
Photos: Courtesy of *The
Sporting News*

ISBN: 1-58261-004-5
Library of Congress Catalog Card Number: 98-86066

SPORTS PUBLISHING INC.
804 N. Neil
Champaign, IL 61820
sportspublishinginc.com

Printed in the United States.

Back cover photo: Matthew McGwire gives his dad, Mark, a high five after McGwire hit his second home run of the night against the Arizona Diamondbacks, Tuesday, April 14, 1998, at Busch Stadium in St. Louis. McGwire hit three home runs against the Diamondbacks that day. (AP photo/Harold Jenkins)

CONTENTS

A portion of the proceeds from the sales of this book will be donated to the MARK McGWIRE FOUNDATION.

Making a Decision

A couple of days after his disappointing 1991 season ended, Mark McGwire got into his car to make the 5 1/2 hour drive from Oakland to Los Angeles, a trip Mark estimates he had made at least 25 times.

As he packed the car, Mark was glad to be putting the worst season of his major-league career behind him. Kids from a school near his home had turned their cheers into taunts. His manager, Tony LaRussa, had intentionally not played him in the

Oakland A's final game, avoiding Mark the embarrassment of seeing his already puny .201 batting average drop below the .200 mark.

Mark's mind was filled with questions and self-doubt. What had happened to the player who had blasted 49 homers as a rookie in 1987? Where was the confidence of the man who put fear into opposing pitchers just because of his 6-foot-5, 225-pound stature? Was he washed up after only six years in the majors?

When Mark slammed the lid of his trunk shut and slid behind the steering wheel, his mind kept racing from one dilemma to the next. For 5 1/2 hours, the entire trip from Oakland to Los Angeles, he faced all of his problems one-by-one as they passed through his mind like the exit signs on the highway.

For the entire trip, Mark never turned on the radio or tape player. He had a built-in sound system that turned the silence of the car into a deafening roar.

When Mark pulled up to a friend's house and got out of the car, his life was about to be changed forever.

"I had to face the music," Mark said. "It was the turning point of my life and it just happened to be the turning point in my career too. No matter who you are in this world, sometimes you have to get slapped in the face. Something has to happen to make you wake up."

For Mark, it was the realization that he wasn't happy. He wasn't enjoying his life, personally or professionally, and he knew he couldn't continue living that way. He had to get help.

"It would have been easy for me to hide and put my head in a hole and sit down and sulk and say 'poor me,'" Mark said. "But I didn't have time to do that. I wanted to turn my life around."

Mark had just celebrated his 28th birthday. A lot of great things had happened in his life. He thought back to his days growing up in southern California, when he often wondered about the future. Suddenly those days didn't seem that long ago.

Growing Up

Mark didn't pay much attention to baseball as a youngster. He remembers playing for the first time when a neighbor was playing and asked Mark to join him. He was eight years old at the time.

Soccer was the most popular sport when Mark was growing up in Claremont, California, a suburb of Los Angeles. He played on a soccer team, and also was introduced to golf at an early age by his father, John, who was a dentist.

A youthful Mark McGwire from his college days at USC.

"I played all the neighborhood sports," Mark says. "It wasn't as organized as it is today."

John was interested in all sports, and had trained as an amateur boxer. He still pounded away on the speed bag in the garage when Mark and his four brothers were growing up.

When John was a boy himself, seven years old, he was forced to spend several months in bed suffering from an illness that left one of his legs much shorter than the other. He never had a chance to play organized sports, but he once did ride a bicycle from San Francisco all the way to San Diego, a distance of more than 500 miles.

John and his wife, Ginger, encouraged their boys to play sports, and they also tried to emphasize the importance of always trying to do their best, no matter if it was in school or an athletic field, to be polite and to respect other people. Those are lessons Mark still tries to follow today.

Three of Mark's four brothers played baseball when they were kids, but all of them gave up the sport by the time they got to high school, prefering to concentrate on other sports. One of his brothers, Dan, became a quarterback at the University of Iowa and San Diego State and was selected in the first round of the NFL draft by the Seattle Seahawks and went on to a pro football career.

One of the reasons Mark was uncertain if he would be able to have much success in sports was because of problems caused by poor eyesight. He recalls having to sit less than a foot in front of the television or he would not have been able to make out the picture. He finally got glasses when he was eight years old.

"I have the worst eyes you could possibly have," Mark says. "No lie. Without contacts or glasses, I can't even see the big E on the eye chart."

Mark began wearing contact lenses when he was a freshman in high school and through a series of eye exercises has improved his vision, with his contacts, to 20-15.

One of the incidents that convinced Mark and his parents that he needed glasses came in one of his early baseball games, when he was pitching. He walked so many batters that his dad, who also was his coach, had him switch places with the shortstop. The view from that position was fuzzy, and Mark had his eyes checked shortly thereafter.

After playing pee-wee ball for a couple of years, Mark joined his first official Little League team when he was 10 years old. He still remembers exactly what happened the first time he came up to bat—he hit a home run.

Mark thought of himself more as a pitcher in those days, however, but he never tried to pattern himself after any major-league player. He enjoyed watching games, and went to the games of the nearby California Angels as much as possible. Mark never had a favorite player or team.

"I'm glad I didn't pay any attention to players when I was a kid," Mark says now. "Today kids pay too much attention to what big league players are like and they want to be like them instead of being themselves. The first and foremost thing is you can only do what God gave you. God didn't give you the ability to copy somebody. He gave you the ability to swing a bat or throw a pitch in your own style.

"That's why I'm glad I didn't sit back and idolize or try to copy somebody when I was a kid."

Even at that early age and lack of experience, Mark's ability was very noticeable to his father.

"The surprising thing was he had an innate sense of how to play," John said. "He knew where to position players, he just knew. It was

After college Mark went on to play for the U.S. team in the 1984 Olympics in Los Angeles.

spinetingling, his understanding of the game at such an early age."

By the time he reached high school, Mark had grown to 6-foot-5 and weighed more than 200 pounds. He had become such a proficient golfer than he had lowered his handicap to 4 and even thought seriously for a while that he would pursue a career in that sport.

Playing golf on such a regular basis began to bore him, however, so Mark turned his attention back to baseball and other sports.

Mark also played basketball at Damien High School in LaVerne, California, and was the starting center on the varsity team for two years. He played mainly because he enjoyed it and because his friends were playing.

Despite his size, Mark didn't play football in high school.

"I thought it was a waste of time to have all of that practice for just one game," Mark said.

It was during his junior year that Mark first began to seriously think he might have a future in baseball. He was drawing attention from some pro scouts and college coaches—as a pitcher.

One of the college coaches who came to watch him was Marcel Lachemann, a future major-league manager who at the time was the pitching coach at the University of Southern California.

"I saw him pitch three times," Lachemann said. "Each time I saw him pitch he hit two home runs. I was looking at him as a pitcher, but you still couldn't discount that."

Lachemann saw enough ability in Mark that he recommended USC offer him a scholarship. Mark's fastball was in the high 80s, and Lachemann thought that with some instructions and refinement Mark would be able to add more velocity and become a better pitcher as he grew older and stronger.

"Everything that I did was totally self-taught," Mark says. "I loved pitching."

The Montreal Expos thought enough of Mark's pitching and hitting ability to make him an eighth-round draft choice after he graduated from high school in 1981. Mark listened to the Expos' offer, but decided he would rather go to college.

Lachemann came to the McGwire home and sold the family on the baseball tradition of USC, where Hall of Famer Tom Seaver had pitched before going on to the major leagues and other future stars had played, like Dave Kingman, Fred Lynn and Steve Kemp.

Mark was convinced, and he was ready to begin his college career.

From College to the Pros

The head baseball coach at USC was Rod Dedeaux, who also was convinced that Mark had a legitimate chance to make it to the major leagues as a pitcher.

"He has a strong arm and an outstanding curveball," Dedeaux said at the time. "His delivery is good and smooth."

McGwire posted a 4-4 record and a 3.04 ERA in 20 games as a freshman. He gave an indication of his offensive ability by hitting three homers.

One of the assistant coaches at USC, Ron Vaughn, was coaching a team in Alaska during the

Mark never gets enough credit for being a good defensive player.

summer of 1982 and he convinced Mark to come and play on his team, the Anchorage Glacier Pilots. Mark thought he was going to work on becoming a better pitcher, but Vaughn had other ideas

— he wanted to turn him into a first baseman.

"That summer was the first time I really ever took hitting seriously," Mark says. "I owe a lot to Ron Vaughn. Basically, he taught me how to stand, hold the bat and hit the ball. He probably knows more about my swing than anybody, even better than I do."

When Mark returned to USC for his sophomore year, and told Dedeaux that he would like to play first base more than pitch, the coach wasn't particularly happy.

Mark's performance during that sophomore year, however, helped to smooth out any hard feelings Dedeaux had for Mark. Mark pitched in only eight games, played the rest at first base, and responded by hitting 19 home runs.

"I remember one scout saying, 'What are you talking about, making him a first baseman?'" Dedeaux said. "'He's a major-league pitcher.' We were just keeping his options open early, until one outshined the other. I think he's still a major league prospect as a pitcher. But with that bat in his hand, he's awesome."

Mark was thinking about a career in baseball, but he also thought about what he might do if he didn't play baseball. He was interested in law enforcement, and he probably would have pursued a career as a police officer if he had not gone into baseball.

Mark was continuing to improve, however, and as a junior he set a school record by blasting 32 homers. His single-season total tied what had been the USC career record. Instead of being projected as a pitcher, Mark now was being watched by scouts ready to select him with their team's first pick in the 1984 draft as a power-hitting first baseman.

Many teams had Mark rated as the top player available in the draft, and the New York Mets, with

the first selection, thought about taking him before selecting a high school outfielder, Shawn Abner.
Mark was not selected until the 10th pick in the
draft, by the Oakland A's.

One of the instructors in the A's organization
didn't think much of Mark's ability and told him so
shortly after the draft.

"He said, 'You'll never be a successful major-
league hitter,'" Mark said. "There's a lot of negativ-
ism in baseball. There's always somebody trying to
put you down. I said to him, 'How do you know? I
haven't been there yet.' I did everything I could to
turn that into a positive."

Before he signed with the A's and began his
professional career, Mark was asked to be a member of the United States team for the 1984 Olympics in Los Angeles, where baseball was being added
as a demonstration sport. The Olympic coach was
Rod Dedeaux, Mark's coach at USC.

Before the Olympics, the talented U.S. team toured the country, playing exhibition games. They played in many major league stadiums, including Fenway Park in Boston, where Mark got to meet future Hall of Famer Reggie Jackson, then playing with the California Angels.

During his game, Mark slammed a home run off the wall behind the centerfield bleachers, a blast estimated at 450 feet. Jackson watched in awe, later calling it "a rocket."

He also watched Mark, who didn't appear to be celebrating the homer. Later, he went up to Mark, introduced himself, and gave him a little friendly advice.

"Son, when you hit a ball like that, you've got to watch it," Jackson told Mark. "No," replied Mark. "That's not my style."

Mark, partly because he had not immersed himself in history books reading about the greats

Playing in the Olympics was a big thrill for Mark and his teammates.

in baseball's past, wasn't too excited when the Olympic team made another stop on its U.S. tour, at baseball's Hall of Fame in Cooperstown, New York.

While many of the players visited the shrine, Mark went to a pizza place with some of his buddies.

The U.S. team was loaded with players who would go on to become successful major leaguers, including Will Clark, Barry Larkin, Cory Snyder, B.J. Surhoff, Billy Swift and Bobby Witt. For Mark, however, the Olympics were a disappointment.

The travel schedule before the Olympics was intense. In a five-week span, the team played 35 games in 33 cities. During one stretch, they played 19 games in 19 cities in as many days. Mark was in New York for the first time in his life, and remembers seeing only the inside of his hotel room and Shea Stadium.

In the Olympics, the team won all of its preliminary games, but lost to Japan, 6-3, in the gold medal game. In five games, Mark posted just a .190 average, going 4-for-21, all singles.

"It was OK, but I was ready to start my career in the minors," Mark said. "If I had been able to play in the minors all year I might have gotten to the major leagues a year earlier."

Mark began his minor-league career in Modesto, California, playing for the A's team in the Class A California League. He played in just 16 games before the season ended, but did produce his first professional home run.

For the start of the 1985 season, the A's wanted Mark to go back to Modesto, but they also wanted to find out if he could play third base, a new position. He quickly showed his offensive prowess, becoming the California League Rookie of the Year by tying for the league lead with 24 homers and 106 RBIs.

**Facing a crowd of reporters and broadcasters is
one of the rituals of the All-Star game's workout
day.**

Defensively, however, Mark had problems at third base, committing 33 errors. He also was developing a reputation as a hot head, a player with a quick temper who would throw bats around whenever a call went against him.

Mark was watching one night when another player lost his temper, and that episode convinced him it was time to change the way he had been acting.

"I saw another player act ridiculous and I looked at myself in the mirror and said, 'I look like that?' Mark said. "From that day on I stopped it. I didn't know I looked that stupid when I was doing that."

The A's promoted Mark to Class AA Huntsville, Alabama, to begin the 1986 season, and he played well, hitting 10 homers, driving in 53 runs and hitting .303 in 55 games. That earned him a mid-season trip to the A's top farm club, Tacoma,

Washington, in the Class AAA Pacific Coast League.

Mark played there for two months, hitting 13 homers, driving in 59 runs and hitting .318 in 78 games before the A's decided he was ready for the next level.

On August 20, Mark got the word that he was heading to the major leagues.

CHAPTER FOUR

A Major Leaguer

Every kid who dreams of playing in the major leagues wonders what that magic moment is going to be like when he steps into the batter's box and collects his first hit.

For Mark, the special feeling came on August 24, 1986, when he delivered a single during the A's game in Yankee Stadium. He had made his major-league debut two days earlier, but had gone hitless in his first two games.

Even without a hit, however, Mark was making a quick impression on the A's and manager Tony

Mark always tries to greet the fans and sign as many autographs as possible.

LaRussa. He hit one drive that was caught just in front of the 410-foot mark in center field.

Mark's first career hit came off veteran Tommy John, who had been a dental patient of Mark's father for several years.

"He used to tell me how good his son was. I thought he was just bragging," John said.

John had been a patient of Dr. McGwire's since 1982, when he was traded to the Angels and had to find a dentist. He remembered Dr. McGwire, whom he had met years earlier during a celebrity golf tournament.

Mark actually collected three hits in the game, adding another single and a double and recording his first RBI.

He had another moment to cherish the next day, playing in Tiger Stadium in Detroit, when he slammed his first career homer against Walt Terrell.

It was a shot to straightaway center field that was measured at 450 feet.

Nobody knew at that point how many more homers were to come. Mark's first exposure to the majors resulted in just a .189 average in 18 games, although he did hit three homers.

The A's were still trying to play Mark at third base, but he made six errors in his six weeks in the majors and before the 1987 season, Mark was moved back to his natural spot at first base.

When Mark reported to spring training, he was hoping he would play well enough to stay in the majors and not have to return to Class AAA. Where to play Mark was a problem for LaRussa, since both Mark and Rob Nelson, another young rookie prospect, were primarily first basemen.

LaRussa decided to keep both young players on his roster when the season began, and platooned them at first base. Neither got off to a great start,

If you don't hit it over the fence, sometimes you have to run hard around the bases and slide into the plate to score a run.

but LaRussa decided to give the majority of the playing time to Mark. On April 20, he called Nelson into his office and gave him the news that he was going back to Tacoma.

Mark was hitting just .167 at the time, but he won the job almost by default when Nelson struggled, striking out in 12 of his 24 at bats.

The decision turned out to be one of the best LaRussa ever made, but he admits at the time it was a lucky move.

Being awarded the full-time job was a boost to Mark's confidence, and it seemed to relax him at the plate. When the A's went to Detroit for a three-game series in early May, the site of Mark's first career homer the previous year, he was ready to explode. In the three games, Mark slammed five home runs.

The onslaught continued for a month, as Mark ripped 15 homers, only one less than Mickey Mantle's major league record for most homers in May. Mark had 20 by June 14, and became the first rookie in history to reach 30 homers before the All-Star break.

By August 11, Mark had tied the record for most homers by a rookie at 38, set by Wally Berger and later matched by Frank Robinson. He broke the mark three days later, with his 39th homer, against Don Sutton.

Attention began to increase, and Mark became a media celebrity. When the A's went to New York and Mark was summoned to a meeting with reporters, he expected to find one or two people waiting. Instead, there was a room filled with reporters, cameras and microphones.

As Mark continued to hit more homers, his notoriety increased even further. His total eventu-

*A three-part
sequence of the
swing: the stance
waiting for the
pitch, making the
perfect swing and
driving the ball
hard, and the follow
through.*

ally reached 49, breaking the team record of 47 that had been set by Reggie Jackson. There was one game left in the season when Mark was awakened in his hotel room in Chicago by an early-morning phone call.

Mark's then wife, Kathy, was calling from Oakland. She was going into labor with the couple's first child. For Mark, there was no hesitation. He caught the first flight back to Oakland, and reached the hospital 45 minutes before his son Matthew was born.

He had missed a chance to become the first rookie in history to hit 50 homers, but he said the birth of his son was the 50th homer.

His son's birth, and being named the unanimous winner of the American League Rookie of the Year award, capped an unbelievable season for Mark.

Among those amazed at what Mark had done were Mark himself and his old college coach, Rod Dedeaux.

"I don't plan things out," Mark said at the time, a philosophy he was to adopt for his entire career as well. "I just go out every day and give my best. I think if you do that, chances are that great things are going to happen. But, yes, I'm completely amazed by all of this. I had no expectations going into this season except to give my all. You know, I was trying just to make the club. I mean, there was major doubt."

Said Dedeaux, "Someone once said to me, 'Did it seem that Tom Seaver would be good enough to be a three-time Cy Young award winner?' Hardly. It's hard to project that. Yes, I was surprised by McGwire. You never expect something like that.

"But I've always felt Mark McGwire would hit home runs in the major leagues and hit many early.

Fans like to see homers, and often asked Mark to make curtain calls out of the dugout after some of his memorable blasts.

He's an intelligent individual. He's got physical talents and more. He's got a good short stroke. He's just a good athlete."

Mark was also smart enough to know that his performance in 1987 was going to bring about higher expectations in 1988 and beyond. He also was smart enough to realize he couldn't expect to have that kind of success every year.

"I remember driving home after games that year and my ex-wife saying, 'We don't know what's going on but go with the ride,'" Mark said. "When I look back on how I did that, it kind of boggles my mind."

Mark was fortunate to have joined the A's just at a time the team was adding some other quality players. Jose Canseco, Dennis Eckersley, Carney Lansford, Dave Stewart and Bob Welch were ready to lead Oakland's pennant drive.

The A's won the American League West title in 1988, the first of three consecutive division titles and American League pennants. Mark's home run total fell to 32, still the third-highest mark in the league, and his biggest blast of the year came in the ninth inning of the third game of the World Series, a solo homer that gave the A's their only victory as they lost the Series to the Dodgers.

Mark hit 33 homers in 1989 to help the A's get back to the World Series, this time playing their rivals from the Bay Area, the San Francisco Giants. The A's won the first two games, then after a day off, were preparing for game three in Candlestick Park when the area was struck by an earthquake.

For Mark, it was a scary experience but not an uncommon one. Having been born and raised in California, Mark knew earthquakes were an almost regular occurrence. "I would rather go through an earthquake than live three or four months in freezing weather in the Midwest and the East," Mark said.

The series was interrupted for 10 days before play resumed. The A's won the next two games, completing a four-game sweep. Almost amazingly, Mark was the only member of the A's regular starting lineup not to hit a homer in the Series.

By the time the A's won the division and pennant for the third consecutive year, in 1990, the team was acting as if it was nothing out of the ordinary. Players walked onto the field to congratulate each other, leaving Mark thinking that the team was taking its success too much for granted.

As a young player, he had been to the World Series three times in his first four seasons in the majors. Some players don't get there once during their entire career.

"When you are a young player you don't really understand it," Mark said. "You are caught up in

The "Bash Brothers," Mark McGwire and Jose Canseco, provided many thrills for the Oakland fans.

such a short time in your career. Later in your career you get wiser and you appreciate the game and how difficult it is to win. When you are younger you just go with the flow."

The team's success was exciting for Mark, but his individual performance was not. His home run total dropped to 22 in 1991 as the A's streak of pennants finally came to an end. Worse, Mark's average fell all the way to .201, prompting many critics to suggest his career was in trouble.

Mark himself had no idea what was wrong, but it was during that long drive after the end of the season that he began to come up with some answers.

CHAPTER FIVE

Rebuilding a Career

Mark's first decision was that he needed counseling, someone he could talk to who would help him come up with solutions for the problems he was having in his personal life.

"People have this thing called pride and sometimes they think they don't want to tell people and that if you go to therapy people will think you're crazy," Mark said. "The people who don't think they have any problems have problems. Everybody has things they can work on and improve on. There's nobody who is perfect in this world."

**Coach Rene Lachemann holds McGwire back after
Mark wanted to go after a pitcher who hit him with
a pitch.**

While the counselor helped Mark correct some of the problems that were affecting him personally, his professional career got a boost because of his improved mental state and from a return to weightlifting and eye exercises designed to improve his vision.

"I realized that your mind controls everything," Mark said. "There are a lot of ballplayers playing this game on strict ability. They don't use their minds. It's amazing to think I played this game for five years without using my mind.

"It was horrible, and yet it was the biggest learning experience of my life, both in baseball and in life. I learned that I had to be who I am, not somebody who somebody else wants me to be."

A new hitting coach, Doug Rader, joined the A's in 1992 and he and Mark immediately developed a good relationship. Mark's work with weights in the winter had added 20 pounds of muscle. Mark knew what he was—a home-run hitter—and his renewed desire helped him increase his homer total to 42, the most he had hit since he was a rookie in 1987.

"I decided I wouldn't fight it because that is what I am, a home run hitter, that's me, that's what God put me here to be," Mark said. "Now, if I get a hit to right field, you can pretty much count on it being an accident."

He was forced to spend three weeks on the disabled list, the start of an injury onslaught that forced Mark to miss 42 percent of the A's games over the next five years. His injuries included a ribcage strain, a torn left heel muscle, a sore lower back, a left heel stress fracture and a torn right heel muscle.

Mark played in only 27 games in 1993 and 47 games in 1994 because of his heel injuries, and he says he wouldn't have been able to overcome such a long period of inactivity if he had not enjoyed the success he had in 1992.

"I wouldn't have had '92 without the bad year of '91," Mark said. "I'm a firm believer that things happen for a reason, and I know that just watching the games those years made me a better hitter. I learned a lot just watching. I learned much more of the mental side. I learned how to stay positive."

That is something Mark says is hard for a lot of players to do, despite the public's perception they have a pretty easy life.

"There are pro ballplayers who are not happy inside," Mark said. "There are a lot of people in general who can't look at themselves in the mirror and say, 'I like myself.' I did, and that was the turning point. My psychiatrist taught me a lot of things about life and myself."

Mark was feeling healthy when the 1995 season began, and the results showed. He hit five hom-

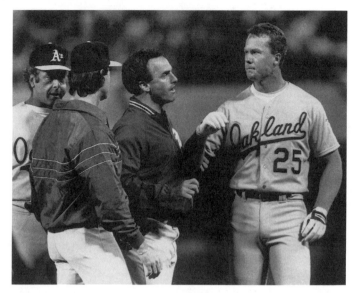

Being hit by a pitch isn't something any player enjoys, and it took trainer Barry Weinberg, manager Tony LaRussa and third base coach Rene Lachemann to calm Mark down after a brush back came too close to him.

ers in a three-game series in Boston in June, joining Ralph Kiner as the only players to hit five homers in two straight games twice in his career. Fans noticed his return, and voted him into the starting lineup for the All-Star game.

Mark was looking forward to the game because it had been three years since his last All-Star appearance. Before the first half of the season ended, however, he had to face Toronto and hard-throwing David Cone, who made a mistake with a fastball and accidentally beaned Mark.

As Mark fell to the ground, the crowd fell silent, fearing Mark had been seriously injured. It turned out Mark suffered only a concussion, but doctors still would not allow him to fly and he was forced to miss the All-Star game.

More injuries cut into Mark's playing time the rest of the season, but he came back to play the final 18 games of the year and slammed 11 homers, raising his season total to 39 despite playing in only 104 games.

When Mark had missed the chance to hit 50 homers in his rookie season so he could be present for the birth of his son, he said there would be other opportunities to hit 50 homers.

As the 1996 season began, there really was no reason to believe this would be the year Mark would prove his nine-year-old statement was correct.

In fact, another injury in spring training—to his right heel—put Mark on the disabled list for the eighth time in his career and prompted him to think about quitting rather than face another long injury rehab. Doctors originally said he could miss as much as three months. Mark's family and friends talked him out of quitting, and Mark made up his mind he would return to action a lot quicker than was expected.

He missed only the first three weeks of the season, and when he returned, began a power assault on American League pitchers. By the end of June he had 25 homers and he added 13 more in July. He finished the month by hitting the longest homer at Toronto's Skydome, a blast into the fifth deck that was measured at 488 feet.

Teammate Scott Brosius was upset after that homer, because he had picked that moment to go into the clubhouse to get something to drink.

"That was my biggest mistake of the season," Brosius said. "It's a mistake ever to miss one of his at-bats. Players aren't usually big fans, but he's a guy you can't help but be in awe of. This guy is the best home-run hitter of them all. He's unbelievable."

Mark's homer total reached 48 on September 7, and the pressure was mounting. He went a week without a homer, going into a doubleheader against Cleveland on September 14.

The drought ended with a first-inning blast off Charles Nagy, matching his personal best of 49 homers. In the second game, he hit number 50 off Chad Ogea.

Gritting your teeth probably doesn't cause the ball to go farther, but it makes a hitter look tougher.

As he rounded the bases, Mark had one thought—he had to get the baseball, because he had promised it to his son Matt. The ball was retrieved from a fan in the stands in exchange for some other memorabilia, and Mark was able to keep his promise.

Mark hit two more homers before the season ended, raising his total to 52, becoming only the 14th player in history to hit 50 or more homers in a season.

Despite his success, the A's front-office executives were faced with a tough decision regarding Mark's contract. He was eligible to become a free agent after the 1997 season, and the team didn't know if it would be able to afford to re-sign him, The team had not won a pennant for several years, attendance had been disappointing, and Mark's performance was going to ensure he received a healthy raise.

Trade rumors began popping up, including one that the A's were perhaps going to deal Mark to the Angels, near his home in southern California. Mark couldn't say anything publicly about the trade talks, but he made it known a trade to the Angels would be fine with him.

The trade talks didn't take away from Mark's concentration on the field, and he continued to blast homers on a regular basis. By the middle of July he had 34, just as the rumors began to intensify.

The trading deadline was July 31, meaning if the A's were going to move Mark to another team they had to do so by that date. Talks were taking place with several teams right up until the deadline when a deal was finally reached with the St. Louis Cardinals. Mark got the news that he had been traded for three pitchers—T.J. Mathews, Eric Ludwick and Blake Stein, a minor-leaguer.

Three consecutive Rookies of the Year wore the Oakland uniform—Jose Canseco, Mark McGwire, and Walt Weiss.

Mark wasn't sure what to think as he prepared to join the Cardinals and leave the A's, but he knew he still was eligible to become a free agent at the end of the season, giving him the option to decide where he wanted to play. His former manager, Tony LaRussa, was now running the Cardinals, and he was willing to go to St. Louis, play out the rest of the season, and see what happened.

Happy as a Cardinal

Leaving the only organization he had known, and going to the National League, was a big change for Mark. It helped that he was going back to playing for LaRussa, and that several of his former teammates were members of the Cardinals, including Dennis Eckersley and Todd Stottlemyre.

At the time of the trade, Mark had 34 homers. There were two months left in the season, but most observers thought all of the changes Mark would have to go through facing new pitchers in a new

*Mark never dreamed he would have so much fun
and adapt to playing in St. Louis so quickly.*

league would rob him of any chance to hit 50 or more homers for the second year in a row.

Mark joined the Cardinals in Philadelphia, and he did get off to a slow start with his new team. He homered in his second at-bat at Busch Stadium on August 8, but in a 27-day span that covered his final days in Oakland and his early days as a Cardinal, Mark hit only two homers.

Going into September, Mark had 43 homers. Any questions about whether or not he could break Roger Maris' mark of 61 homers definitely had faded away.

Perhaps because of the lack of pressure, Mark went on a home-run binge in the final month. He blasted 15 homers, breaking the Cardinals' record for most homers in a month, and allowing him to match Jimmie Foxx's and Hank Greenberg's record for most homers in a season by a righthanded batter, 58.

He became the only player other than Babe Ruth to hit 50 or more in consecutive seasons, and he became the first player in history to hit 20 or more homers for two teams in the same season.

Mark also became, in almost an instant, one of the biggest sports celebrities to ever come onto the St. Louis scene.

Watching Mark take batting practice, and seeing him smash ball after ball into the upper deck, became the "in" thing in town. The Cardinals were forced to open the gates to the ballpark earlier than normal to allow fans to enter while Mark was still taking BP. There actually was a documented case of one fan purchasing a ticket to the game, coming in for batting practice to watch Mark, and then leaving to attend a Rams' pre-season football game.

Mark was overwhelmed by his sudden stardom. He couldn't understand the fascination fans had for

Mark says hitting a home run might be the hardest thing to do in sports.

watching him take batting practice, a routine he hadn't changed in his 14 years in the majors.

"I never realized the support of a true fan until I got to St. Louis," Mark said. "I used the word overwhelming a lot. This is the way people are supposed to treat their teams."

When he was traded, Mark had fully intended to use his two months in St. Louis as an evaluation period, to see if he liked the city and the team and to see if the people liked him. He knew he would consider an offer from the Cardinals in the winter because of LaRussa, but he also was hoping a team in southern California would make an offer, allowing him to play at home and spend more time with his son Matt.

His success, however, and the way he was welcomed and received into the city, changed those plans. He called his attorney in mid-September and told him to work out a contract with the Cardinals. He wanted to stay.

Mark knew he probably could have received more money if he had waited until the winter and allowed other teams to bid for his services, but his mind was made up. The negotations were short, and Mark signed a new three-year contract.

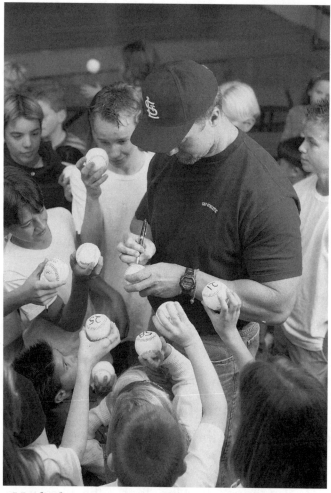

Mark always tries to accommodate his fans as much as possible.

If Mark thought the fans in St. Louis had been kind to him before, he saw an even higher level of support and appreciation after the new agreement was announced. The contract was signed on September 16, hours before the Cardinals played host to Los Angeles.

At the news conference announcing the new deal, Mark broke down when it was revealed that he would be donating $1 million a year to a new foundation he was establishing to help physically and sexually abused children.

When Mark came up to bat in the first inning that night, the fans were on their feet roaring— even before he launched a towering 517-foot rocket off the facade above the scoreboard in left center field—at the time the longest homer ever measured at Busch Stadium.

It also didn't take Mark long to begin to appreciate the rich baseball tradition in St. Louis, which

Mark is all smiles in Cardinal red these days.

has been home to a major-league team for more than 100 years.

Mark hadn't been in St. Louis for long when he was summoned into LaRussa's office before a game. "Mark, I'd like you to meet somebody," LaRussa said. "Mark, this is Stan Musial."

"All of the Hall of Famers they have in St. Louis means something to me," Mark said. "It's nice to be able to have a one-on-one conversation with them. You can appreciate everything they went through in their career."

For his success on the field and his charity involvement off the field, Mark was named the 1997 Sportsman of the Year by *The Sporting News.*

Mark's popularity increased even more, if that was possible, during the early days of the 1998 season. He blasted a grand slam on opening day, the first Cardinal ever to do that, and proceeded to homer in the next three games as well. One of the

*A familiar sight—Mark being greeted by a
teammate after hitting another home run.*

blasts was a game-winning homer in the 12th, and he matched Willie Mays' record of homering in the first four games of the season.

It seemed as if everybody in St. Louis was wearing a red jersey with "McGwire 25" on the back, and his accomplishments were the talk of the town.

All of that attention still makes Mark very uncomfortable.

"You don't play this game to get attention," Mark said. "You play this game because you are talented and you are good at it, and it's fun. I don't know anybody when they start playing as a kid who says, 'I want to play so I can get my name in the newspaper.' You play because you enjoy the game."

About the only aspect of the game that Mark doesn't enjoy is the way all professional athletes are turned into "role models" for young people.

"My theory on this is that you don't know an athlete's background," Mark said. "You don't know where he grew up, you don't know what kind of family he came from. All of a sudden he might do something wrong, which he could have been doing his whole life, and people say 'what a bad role model he is.' Maybe he wasn't a role model in the first place. Don't put that label on him."

What Mark does want is for kids to play baseball, and to have fun doing it. Part of his approach to the game, and no doubt part of the secret to his success, is that he still brings a child-like enthusiasm with him to the ballpark every day.

"I'm realistic." Mark said. "It's just a game. You can approach it that way if you understand that millions of kids would love to be in the situation that you're in, and that you're blessed to have the opportunity to do it. The bottom line is to have fun. I enjoy my work and I work hard."

When Mark sees somebody who doesn't share his appreciation for the game, it bothers him.

"I enjoy watching other players play, especially people that I know," Mark said. "I love the game."

Cardinal fans hope Mark has a lot to smile about in the upcoming seasons.

On Hitting 62

Mark believes that hitting a home run might be the hardest thing to do in sports.

"You get in the box, you see the ball as best you can, you react to it and try to hit it," Mark said. "If it leaves the ballpark, great. If it's a base hit, great. If it's a strikeout, you learn from it. It's not like somebody is putting the ball on the tee for you and saying, 'Here, hit it over the fence.'"

Mark's 58 homers in 1997, and the 56 hit by Seattle's Ken Griffey Jr., convinced Mark and most

other observers that Roger Maris' record of 61 homers in a season could be broken.

Before the 1998 season began, Mark said that if hitting 61 homers were easy, people wouldn't be talking about it or asking him what he thought his chances were of getting the record.

"A season has to be absolutely perfect for it to happen," Mark said in spring training. "I'm not saying I can do it. I'm not saying I can't. It's not worth talking about until someone goes into September with 50."

Entering the 1998 season, Mark had averaged one home run for every 11.94 at-bats during his career. The only player in history with a better ratio was Babe Ruth.

Mark began the year with a bang. His grand slam on opening day carried the Cardinals to a victory over the Los Angeles Dodgers. He followed that blast by hitting homers in each of his next three

games, matching Willie Mays' National League record of homering in the season's first four games.

The talk that Mark was going to break Maris' record was already increasing, and the season was less than a week old.

"It's made baseball a little more exciting to think about it and talk about it," Mark said. "But if you really look at it, ever since I was a kid, what do you go to the ballpark for? You go to the ballpark to see somebody hit a home run or somebody throw a ball at close to 100 miles per hour. That was an exciting thing when I was a kid and I still think is."

Mark thinks the biggest key to hitting home runs is just being born with natural ability.

"Every year adults ask me, 'Can you teach my son how to hit home runs?'" Mark said. "And I say. 'No, I can't.' I think you're given the talent. If you want to work on it, then you become a successful baseball player. It's just a tough thing."

Mark said he knows there are players whom he played with and against in high school who think the only reason Mark made it to the majors and they didn't is luck.

"I'm sure they are sitting on their couch at home now saying they could have made it," Mark said. "You know who stopped them? Themselves. That's what stops kids today. Nobody stops them but themselves."

The best advice Mark tries to give kids is to set no limits on what they can accomplish and also to be themselves. It took him a long time to figure out that he is supposed to be a home-run hitter.

"God gives you something at birth," Mark said. "You are on this earth to try to figure out what it is. It's not to copy somebody's swing or jump shot or the way he passes the football or the way he runs with the football. You have to be yourself. So many children today try not being themselves and that's why they get in trouble. When they don't succeed trying to be somebody else, then they walk away from the game. They say, 'I'm not any good.' How do they know?"

Mark found out just how good he could be in 1998. With his son Matthew in town on April 14, Mark pounded three homers in a game against the Arizona Diamondbacks. On May 16, against Florida, he hit the longest homer ever in Busch Stadium. The blast, off a sign in center field, was measured at 545 feet.

On May 19 at Philadelphia, Mark repeated his three-homer feat, becoming only the 12th player in history to have two three-homer games in the same season.

By the end of June, Mark had 37 homers, tying the record for most homers before the All-Star break.

His assault on National League pitchers continued after the break, but with an added bonus. Another player, the Cubs' Sammy Sosa, was keeping pace with Mark and making their two-man race more exciting than most pennant races.

On August 19 in Chicago, Sammy hit his 48th homer to pass Mark and take over the lead. Sammy's lead ended 57 minutes later, when Mark responded with his 48th. Two innings later, Mark homered again and was back on top.

The next night in New York, Mark ripped his 50th homer, becoming the first player in history to hit 50 or more homers in three consecutive seasons.

Reaching that milestone seemed to relax Mark, and he finished August with 55 homers, just seven away from the magic number.

In back-to-back games at Florida to begin September, Mark hit two homers in each game. Suddenly, he was on the verge of history.

On September 5 against Cincinnati, Mark became the first player since Maris to reach the 60-homer mark with a 381-foot shot over the left field wall.

Two days later, going head-to-head against Sosa, Mark tied Maris with his 61st blast off Mike Morgan of the Cubs. The blast came on Mark's father's 61st birthday. The next night, with more than 700 reporters from all over the world on hand, Mark faced the pressure of needing one more homer to break the record.

In his second at-bat of the game, the pressure evaporated. Mark's fly ball off Steve Trachsel barely cleared the left field wall—ironically his shortest homer of the season—and Mark was the new home run champion.

The homer ignited a tremendous celebration, which included Mark going into the stands to hug Maris' children, who had made the trip from Florida for the momentous occasion.

Mark hit homer number 61 on his father's 61st birthday.

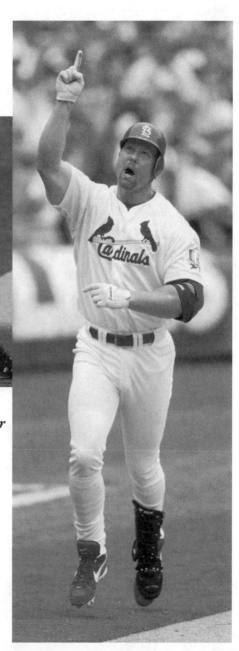

Mark's record-breaking 62nd home run against Steve Trachsel set off a wild celebration with fans as Mark celebrated with his son Matt (right).

Sosa, the competitor who had become a friend, stood in right field applauding, then jogged in and hugged Mark in a great display of sportsmanship (photo at right). Also on hand was Mark's son, Matt, who had arrived from California the day before. The picture of Mark picking up Matt and lifting him into the air was on the front page of newspapers all over the world the following morning.

"It's such an incredible feeling," Mark said. "I can't believe I did it."

Mark had earned his place in the history books. There still wasn't time to stop and enjoy the moment, however. He still had more games to play.

Epilogue

Mark's 62nd homer made him a national celebrity, putting his picture on the cover of magazines and making his accomplishment the top story on broadcasts around the world. He now owned one of the most heralded records in sports and was being recognized for it.

Almost lost in the attention, however, was the fact that with 58 homers of his own, Sosa still was in a position where he also could break the record and perhaps end up passing Mark.

Possibly because of all of the attention and the emotional letdown that followed the 62nd homer, Mark went a week before he homered again, hitting a homer as a pinch-hitter on September 15 against Pittsburgh.

Sosa was closing the gap, as he also reached the 60-mark, then followed with his 61st and 62nd blasts. In his homeland of the Dominican Republic, the celebration that followed rivaled that of Mark's fans in St. Louis.

Mark hit his 64th and 65th homers in a series at Milwaukee, and as the season entered its final week, he had two-homer edge over Sosa. The 65th was special for Mark because that was the number his son Matt had told him in spring training he wanted Mark to hit during the season.

Mark's margin over Sosa didn't last long, as Sosa belted two homers in a game at Milwaukee on September 23 to put the two sluggers in a tie at 65 with three games remaining.

Playing in Houston on September 25, Sosa fired the next shot, blasting a homer into the upper deck at the Astrodome to knock Mark out of the top spot. As had been the case when Sosa had passed Mark in the game in Chicago five weeks earlier, the lead didn't last very long.

Sammy Sosa hits No. 66 to keep the home run race exciting.

This time, Sosa was ahead in the home run race for 45 minutes, before Mark sent his 66th homer into the seats in left field.

That homer ignited a tremendous final week-
end for Mark. On the last two days of the season,
he hit four more homers, two in each game, and
finished the year with the almost-unheard of total
of 70 home runs. Sosa finished with 66, although
he got to play an extra game as the Cubs needed a
playoff game to break a tie with the San Francisco
Giants for the NL's wildcard entry in the postseason.

After the final homer, which came in his final
at-bat and gave him five homers in his last 11 at-bats
of the season, Mark still was having a little trouble
trying to digest everything that had happened since
March.

"This is a season I will never, ever forget and I
hope everybody in baseball never forgets," Mark
said.

Never in his wildest dreams could he imagine
hitting 70 homers in a season. But that's exactly
what he did.

"I think the magnitude of this probably won't sink in for a while," Mark said. "I'm like in awe of myself right now."

Mark's accomplishment will make it hard for him to not look back at the past, but keep focusing on the future, something he always has been able to do extremely well.

"I'm a firm believer that people who live in the past never succeed in anything," Mark said. "They're always failing."

That isn't something Mark has to ever worry about.

Mark McGwire Statistics

Complete Record

Year	Club	AVG.	G	AB	R	H	2B	3B	HR	RBI	BB	SO	SB
1984	Modesto	.200	16	55	7	11	3	0	1	1	8	21	0
1985	Modesto	.274	138	489	95	134	23	3	+24	+106	96	108	1
1986	Huntsville	.303	55	195	40	59	15	0	10	53	46	45	3
	Tacoma	.318	78	280	42	89	21	5	13	59	42	67	1
	Oakland	.189	18	53	10	10	1	0	3	9	4	18	0
1987	Oakland	.289	151	557	97	161	28	4	*49	118	71	131	1
1988	Oakland	.260	155	550	87	143	22	1	32	99	76	117	0
1989	Oakland	.231	143	490	74	113	17	0	33	95	83	94	1
1990	Oakland	.235	156	523	87	123	16	0	39	108	*110	116	2
1991	Oakland	.201	154	483	62	97	22	0	22	75	93	116	2
1992	Oakland	.268	139	467	87	125	22	0	42	104	90	105	0
1993	Oakland	.333	27	84	16	28	6	0	9	24	21	19	0
1994	Oakland	.252	47	135	26	34	3	0	9	25	37	40	0
1995	Oakland	.274	104	317	75	87	13	0	39	90	88	77	1
1996	Oakland	.312	130	423	104	132	21	0	*52	113	116	112	0
1997	Oakland	.284	105	366	48	104	24	0	34	81	58	98	1
	St. Louis	.253	51	174	38	44	3	0	24	42	43	61	2
1998	St. Louis	.299	155	509	130	152	21	0	*70	147	*162	155	1
A.L. Totals		.260	1329	4448	773	1157	195	5	363	941	847	1043	8
N.L. Totals		.287	206	683	168	196	24	0	94	189	205	216	3
Major League Totals		.264	1535	5131	941	1353	219	5	457	1130	1052	1259	11

*Led league
+Tied for league lead

League Championhip Series Record

Year	Club/Opp.	AVG.	G	AB	R	H	2B	3B	HR	RBI	BB	SO	SB
1988	Oak. vs. Bos.	.333	4	15	4	5	0	0	1	3	1	5	0
1989	Oak. vs. Tor.	.389	5	18	3	7	1	0	1	3	1	4	0
1990	Oak. vs. Bos.	.154	4	13	2	2	0	0	0	2	3	3	0
1992	Oak. vs. Tor.	.150	6	20	1	3	0	0	1	3	5	4	0
L.C.S. totals		.258	19	66	10	17	1	0	3	11	10	16	0

World Series Record

Year	Club/Opp.	AVG.	G	AB	R	H	2B	3B	HR	RBI	BB	SO	SB
1988	Oak. vs. LA.	.059	5	17	1	1	0	0	1	1	3	4	0
1989	Oak. vs. S.F.	.294	4	17	0	5	1	0	0	1	1	3	0
1990	Oak. vs. Cin.	.214	4	14	1	3	0	0	0	0	2	4	0
W.S. totals		.188	13	48	2	9	1	0	1	2	6	11	0

All-Star Game Record

Year	Club/Opp.	AVG.	G	AB	R	H	2B	3B	HR	RBI	BB	SO	SB
1987	American	.000	1	3	0	0	0	0	0	0	0	0	0
1988	American	.500	1	2	0	1	0	0	0	0	0	1	0
1989	American	.333	1	3	0	1	0	0	0	0	0	0	0
1990	American	.000	1	2	0	0	0	0	0	0	0	2	0
1991	American	Selected, did not play											
1992	American	.333	1	3	1	1	0	0	0	2	0	0	0
1995	American	Selected, did not play											
1996	American	1.000	1	1	0	1	0	0	0	0	0	0	0
1997	American	.000	1	2	0	0	0	0	0	0	0	2	0
1998													
All-Star totals		.250	7	16	1	4	0	0	0	2	0	5	0

Mark McGwire-Career Transactions

- Selected by Montreal Expos in eighth round of June 1981 free-agent draft

- Selected by Oakland A's in first round (tenth player selected) of June 1984 free-agent draft

- Acquired by St. Louis Cardinals in a trade with Oakland A's for pitchers T.J. Mathews, Eric Ludwick and Blake Stein, July 31, 1997.

Mark McGwire's 70 Home Runs in 1998

No.	Date	Opponent	Pitcher	Inn.	Outs	Count	RBI	Dist.	Direction
1.	3/31	LA	Ramon Martinez	5	2	1-0	4	364	left
2.	4/2	LA	Frank Lankford	12	2	0-1	3	368	left-center
3.	4/3	SD	Mark Langston	5	0	3-2	2	364	left
4.	4/4	SD	Don Wengert	6	0	2-1	3	419	center
5.	4/14	Ariz	Jeff Suppan	3	1	1-2	2	424	left
6.	4/14	Ariz	Jeff Suppan	5	2	1-1	1	347	left
7.	4/14	Ariz	Barry Manuel	8	0	2-0	2	462	center
8.	4/17	Phi	Matt Whiteside	4	2	2-2	2	419	left-center
9.	4/21	Mon	Trey Moore	3	2	0-0	2	437	left-center
10.	4/25	Phi	Jerry Spradlin	7	2	1-2	2	419	center
11.	4/30	ChN	Marc Pisciotta	8	1	2-1	2	371	left-center
12.	5/1	ChN	Rod Beck	9	2	1-2	2	362	left-center
13.	5/8	NYN	Rick Reed	3	1	0-2	2	358	left
14.	5/12	Mil	Paul Wagner	5	0	1-2	3	527	left-center
15.	5/14	Atl	Kevin Millwood	4	0	1-1	1	381	right-center
16.	5/16	Fla	Livan Hernandez	4	0	1-0	1	545	center
17.	5/18	Fla	Jesus Sanchez	4	0	2-0	1	478	left
18.	5/19	Phi	Tyler Green	3	1	2-0	2	440	center
19.	5/19	Phi	Tyler Green	5	0	0-2	2	471	left-center
20.	5/19	Phi	Wayne Gomes	8	0	0-0	2	451	left-center
21.	5/22	SF	Mark Gardner	6	1	1-1	2	425	left
22.	5/23	SF	Rich Rodriguez	4	1	1-0	1	366	left
23.	5/23	SF	John Johnstone	5	1	2-2	3	477	left-center
24.	5/24	SF	Robb Nen	12	2	2-2	2	397	left
25.	5/25	Col	John Thomson	1	2	2-2	1	433	left
26.	5/29	SD	Dan Miceli	9	1	0-1	2	388	left-center
27.	5/30	SD	Andy Ashby	1	2	0-1	1	423	center
28.	6/5	SF	Orel Hershiser	1	1	1-2	2	409	center
29.	6/8	ChA	Jason Bere	4	0	0-0	2	356	left
30.	6/10	ChA	Jim Parque	3	1	1-0	3	409	center
31.	6/12	Ariz	Andy Benes	3	1	1-0	4	438	left-center
32.	6/17	Hou	Jose Lima	3	2	1-2	1	347	left
33.	6/18	Hou	Shane Reynolds	5	0	1-1	1	449	left-center
34.	6/24	Cle	Jaret Wright	4	1	1-1	1	433	left

No.	Date	Opponent	Pitcher	Inn.	Outs	Count	RBI	Dist.	Direction
35.	6/25	Cle	Dave Burba	1	2	2-2	1	461	left
36.	6/27	Min	Mike Trombley	7	2	2-2	2	431	left-center
37.	6/30	KC	Glendon Rusch	7	0	0-1	1	472	left
38.	7/11	Hou	Billy Wagner	11	1	0-2	2	485	left
39.	7/12	Hou	Sean Bergman	1	2	0-0	1	405	left
40.	7/12	Hou	Scott Elarton	7	0	2-1	1	415	left
41.	7/17	LA	Brian Bohanon	1	2	0-0	1	511	left
42.	7/17	LA	Antonio Osuna	8	1	1-0	1	425	left
43.	7/20	SD	Brian Boehringer	5	0	2-1	2	458	left-center
44.	7/26	Col	John Thomson	4	2	0-0	1	452	left
45.	7/28	Mil	Mike Myers	8	1	2-2	1	408	right-center
46.	8/8	ChN	Mark Clark	4	0	2-1	1	374	left
47.	8/11	NYN	Bobby Jones	4	0	1-0	1	464	left-center
48.	8/19	ChN	Matt Karchner	8	1	3-1	1	430	left
49.	8/19	ChN	Terry Mulholland	10	1	2-0	1	402	center
50.	8/20	NYN	Willie Blair	7	0	2-1	1	385	left
51.	8/20	NYN	Rick Reed	1	2	3-2	1	369	left
52.	8/22	Pit	Francisco Cordova	1	2	0-2	1	477	right-center
53.	8/23	Pit	Ricardo Rincon	8	2	2-2	1	393	left
54.	8/26	Fla	Justin Speier	8	0	0-1	2	509	center
55.	8/30	Atl	Dennis Martinez	7	0	1-0	3	501	center
56.	9/1	Fla	Livan Hernandez	7	0	1-1	1	450	center
57.	9/1	Fla	Donn Pall	9	1	0-0	1	472	center
58.	9/2	Fla	Brian Edmondson	7	2	2-1	2	497	left
59.	9/2	Fla	Robby Stanifer	8	2	0-0	2	458	left-center
60.	9/5	Cin	Dennis Reyes	1	1	2-0	2	381	left
61.	9/7	ChN	Mike Morgan	1	2	1-1	1	430	left
62.	9/8	ChN	Steve Trachsel	4	2	0-0	1	341	left
63.	9/15	Pit	Jason Christiansen	9	1	0-1	1	385	left-center
64.	9/18	Mil	Rafael Roque	4	0	3-1	2	417	left-center
65.	9/20	Mil	Scott Karl	1	1	2-1	2	423	left-center
66.	9/25	Mon	Shayne Bennett	5	2	1-2	2	375	left
67.	9/26	Mon	Dustin Hermanson	4	1	0-0	1	403	left-center
68.	9/26	Mon	Kirk Bullinger	7	2	1-1	2	435	center
69.	9/27	Mon	Mike Thurman	3	2	1-1	1	377	left
70.	9/27	Mon	Carl Pavano	7	2	0-0	3	370	left

Career Home Run Leaders
(Through 1998 season)

1.	Hank Aaron	755
2.	Babe Ruth	714
3.	Willie Mays	660
4.	Frank Robinson	586
5.	Harmon Killebrew	573
6.	Reggie Jackson	563
7.	Mike Schmidt	548
8.	Mickey Mantle	536
9.	Jimmie Foxx	534
10.	Willie McCovey	521
	Ted Williams	521
12.	Ernie Banks	512
	Eddie Mathews	512
14.	Mel Ott	511
15.	Eddie Murray	504
16.	Lou Gehrig	493
17.	Stan Musial	475
	Willie Stargell	475
19.	Dave Winfield	465
20.	**x-MARK McGWIRE**	**457**
21.	Carl Yastrzemski	452
22.	Dave Kingman	442
23.	Andre Dawson	438
24.	Billy Williams	426
25.	Darrell Evans	414
26.	x-Barry Bonds	411
27.	Duke Snider	407
28.	Al Kaline	399
29.	Dale Murphy	398
30.	x-Jose Canseco	397

x-active

Active Home Run Leaders
(Through 1998 season)

1.	**MARK McGWIRE**	**457**
2.	Barry Bonds	411
3.	Jose Canseco	397
4.	Joe Carter	396
5.	Cal Ripken Jr.	384
6.	Fred McGriff	358
7.	Gary Gaetti	351
8.	Ken Griffey Jr.	350
9.	Harold Baines	348
10.	Darryl Strawberry	332
	Andres Galarraga	332

Career Home Run—American League
(Through 1998 season)

1.	Babe Ruth	708
2.	Harmon Killebrew	573
3.	Reggie Jackson	563
4.	Mickey Mantle	536
5.	Jimmie Foxx	524
6.	Ted Williams	521
7.	Lou Gehrig	493
8.	Carl Yastrzemski	452
9.	Al Kaline	399
10.	Eddie Murray	396
17.	**MARK McGWIRE**	**363**

Career At-Bats Per Home Run
(Min. 250 HR, Through 1998 season)

1.	**MARK McGWIRE**	**5131**	**457**	**11.23**
2.	Babe Ruth	8399	714	11.76
3.	Ralph Kiner	5205	369	14.11
4.	Juan Gonzalez	4269	301	14.18
5.	Harmon Killebrew	8147	573	14.22
6.	Albert Belle	4684	321	14.59
7.	Ted Williams	7706	521	14.79
8.	Ken Griffey Jr.	5226	350	14.93
9.	Dave Kingman	6677	442	15.11
10.	Mickey Mantle	8102	536	15.12

Career Home Runs, Righthander
(Through 1998 season)

1.	Hank Aaron	755
2.	Willie Mays	660
3.	Frank Robinson	586
4.	Harmon Killebrew	573
5.	Mike Schmidt	548
6.	Jimmie Foxx	534
7.	Ernie Banks	512
8.	Dave Winfield	465
9.	**MARK McGWIRE**	**457**
10.	Dave Kingman	442

Career Home Runs, First Baseman
(Through 1998 season)

1.	Lou Gehrig	493
2.	Jimmie Foxx	480
3.	**MARK MCGWIRE**	**443**
4.	Willie McCovey	439
5.	Eddie Murray	409
6.	Norm Cash	367
7.	Johnny Mize	350
8.	Gil Hodges	335
9.	Fred McGriff	298
10.	Orlando Cepeda	293

Career 30-Home Run Seasons
(Through 1998 season)

1.	Hank Aaron	15
2.	Babe Ruth	13
	Mike Schmidt	13
4.	Jimmie Foxx	12
5.	Willie Mays	11
	Frank Robinson	11
7.	Lou Gehrig	10
	Harmon Killebrew	10
	Eddie Mathews	10
10.	**MARK McGWIRE**	**9**
	Mickey Mantle	9

Career Multiple Home Run Games
(Through 1998 season)

1.	Babe Ruth	72
2.	Willie Mays	63
3.	Hank Aaron	62
4.	Jimmie Foxx	55
5.	Frank Robinson	54
6.	**MARK McGWIRE**	**53**
7.	Eddie Mathews	49
	Mel Ott	49
9.	Harmon Killebrew	46
	Mickey Mantle	46

Career Slugging Percentage
(Minimum 2,000 total bases, Through 1998 season)

1.	Babe Ruth	.690
2.	Ted Williams	.634
3.	Lou Gehrig	.632
4.	Jimmie Foxx	.609
5.	Hank Greenberg	.605
6.	Frank Thomas	.600
7.	Joe DiMaggio	.579
8.	Rogers Hornsby	.577
	Albert Belle	.577
10.	**MARK McGWIRE**	**.576**

Home Runs (season)

1.	**MARK McGWIRE, Cardinals, 1998**	**70**
2.	Sammy Sosa, Cubs, 1998	66
3.	Roger Maris, Yankees, 1961	61
4.	Babe Ruth, Yankees, 1927	60
5.	Babe Ruth, Yankees, 1921	59
6.	Jimmie Foxx, A's, 1932	58
	Hank Greenberg, Tigers, 1938	58
	MARK McGWIRE, A'S-CARDINALS, 1997	**58**
9.	Hack Wilson, Cubs, 1930	56
	Ken Griffey Jr., Mariners, 1998	56
	Ken Griffey Jr., Mariners, 1997	56
12.	Ralph Kiner, Pirates, 1949	54
	Mickey Mantle, Yankees, 1961	54
	Babe Ruth, Yankees, 1920	54
	Babe Ruth, Yankees, 1928	54
16.	George Foster, Reds, 1977	52
	Mickey Mantle, Yankees, 1956	52
	Willie Mays, Giants, 1965	52
	MARK McGWIRE, A'S, 1996	**52**

Home Runs Righthander (season)

1.	**MARK McGWIRE, CARDINALS**	**70**
2.	Sammy Sosa, Cubs	66
3.	Jimmie Foxx, A's, 1932	58
	Hank Greenberg, Tigers, 1938	58
	MARK McGWIRE, A'S-CARDINALS	**58**
6.	Hack Wilson, Cubs, 1930	56
7.	Ralph Kiner, Pirates, 1949	54
8.	George Foster, Reds, 1977	52
	Willie Mays, Giants, 1965	52
	MARK McGWIRE, A'S, 1996	**52**
11.	Cecil Fielder, Tigers, 1990	51
	Ralph Kiner, Pirates, 1947	51
	Willie Mays, Giants, 1955	51
14.	Albert Belle, Indians, 1995	50
	Jimmie Foxx, Red Sox, 1938	50

Home Runs First Baseman (season)

1.	**MARK McGWIRE, CARDINALS, 1998**	**70**
2.	Hank Greenberg, Tigers, 1938	58
3.	**MARK McGWIRE, A'S-CARDINALS, 1997**	**57**
4.	Jimmie Foxx, A's, 1932	51
	Johnny Mize, Giants, 1947	51
6.	Jimmie Foxx, Red Sox, 1938	50
7.	Lou Gehrig, Yankees, 1934	49
	Lou Gehrig, Yankees, 1936	49
	Ted Kluszewski, Reds, 1954	49
10.	Jimmie Foxx, A's, 1933	48
	MARK McGWIRE, A'S, 1987	**48**
	Cecil Fielder, Tigers, 1990	48